Time to Celebrate!

LET'S GO TO A HALLOWEEN PARTY!

I0813896

By Benjamin Proudfit

Please visit our website, www.garethstevens.com. For a free color catalog of all our high-quality books, call toll free 1-800-542-2595 or fax 1-877-542-2596.

Library of Congress Cataloging-in-Publication Data

Names: Proudfit, Benjamin.
Title: Let's go to a Halloween party! / Benjamin Proudfit.
Description: New York : Gareth Stevens Publishing, 2020. | Series: Time to celebrate!
Identifiers: ISBN 9781538238943 (pbk.) | ISBN 9781538238967 (library bound) | ISBN 9781538238950 (6 pack)
Subjects: LCSH: Halloween–Juvenile fiction. | Parties–Juvenile fiction.
Classification: LCC PZ7.P768 Le 2020 | DDC [E]–dc23

First Edition

Published in 2020 by
Gareth Stevens Publishing
111 East 14th Street, Suite 349
New York, NY 10003

Editor: Kristen Nelson
Designer: Katelyn E. Reynolds

Photo credits: Cover, p. 1 Roman Samborskyi/Shutterstock.com; p. 5 Yuganov Konstantin/Shutterstock.com; p. 7 Mike Flippo/Shutterstock.com; p. 9 gpointstudio/Shutterstock.com; pp. 11, 23, 24 (costume) Rawpixel.com/Shutterstock.com; p. 13 Monkey Business Images/Shutterstock.com; p. 15 5 second Studio/Shutterstock.com; p. 17 Sean Locke Photography/Shutterstock.com; pp. 19, 24 (haunted house) Africa Studio/Shutterstock.com; p. 21 tetxu/Shutterstock.com.

Printed in the United States of America

CPSIA compliance information: Batch #CS19GS: For further information contact Gareth Stevens, New York, New York at 1-800-542-2595.

Contents

Halloween is my
favorite holiday!
I am having a party.

We put up orange lights.

My sister puts out candy.
It is like trick-or-treating!

Everyone wears
a costume.

Daphne dresses
as a cat.

Lawrence is a monster.

We bob for apples.
Ganon’s face gets wet!

Leah is scared!

What will you do at your Halloween party?

Words to Know

costume

haunted house

Index